PARENT'S SHELF

E

Pirates Can Be Honest

Tom Easton

WINDMILL BOOKS

New York

Published in 2016 by **Windmill Books**, an Imprint of Rosen Publishing

29 East 21st Street, New York, NY 10010

Commissioning editor: Victoria Brooker
Creative design: Basement68
Illustrations© Mike Gordon

Manufactured in
the United States of America

CPSIA Compliance Information: Batch #BW16PK:
For Further Information contact Rosen Publishing,
New York, New York at 1-800-237-9932

Cataloging-in-Publication Data

Easton, Tom.
Pirates can be honest / by Tom Easton.
p. cm. — (Pirate pals)
Includes index.
ISBN 978-1-5081-9141-4 (pbk.)
ISBN 978-1-5081-9142-1 (6-pack)
ISBN 978-1-5081-9143-8 (library binding)
1. Honesty — Juvenile fiction. I. Easton,
Tom (Children's fiction writer). II. Title.
PZ7.E13159 Pir 2016
[F]—d23

Pirates Can Be Honest

Written by
Tom Easton

Illustrated by
Mike Gordon

WINDMILL
BOOKS ™

New York

Some days you're better off just staying
in bed. But staying in bed wasn't an option
for poor old Davy Jones the day his hammock
snapped! His day soon got worse.

Captain Cod asked Davy to clean
the cannonballs belowdecks.
"But, Captain," Davy said. "Cleaning
cannonballs is the worst job on the ship."

"Sorry, Davy," the Captain said, "but if there's
one thing I insist on, it's clean cannonballs.
Be careful that you don't drop any!"

Davy went down into the hold and sighed
as he saw the huge pile of cannonballs.
"They're heavy and greasy and there are
just so many of them," he said to himself.
"This is going to take forever!"

But there was nothing else to do.
Davy got to work. He scrubbed, spat
and shined. As the cannonballs
got cleaner, he got dirtier.

As the day went on, Davy grew hungry and tired.
He began daydreaming about having
a nice bubble bath before dinner. In fact,
Davy was so busy daydreaming, he dropped
a particularly heavy cannonball on his big toe.

Davy hopped around clutching
his foot and saying some rude words.
Meanwhile, the cannonball rolled right
through an open hatch in the floor.

Davy rushed to see. Uh-oh! The cannonball had fallen right down into the hold and through the hull.

Water bubbled up through the hole it had made.

Just then, Davy heard
the Captain coming. In a panic,
he closed the hatch.

"Everything OK, Davy?"
the Captain asked.

"Err, yes, Cap'n," Davy replied.
"Nearly finished."

"Arr. Well done," the Captain replied.
"I do like a clean cannonball. There'll be extra
sausages for you tonight. Come on, leave
the rest. Let's go and eat."

But Davy couldn't eat. He was worried about the leak in the hold. Why hadn't he told the Captain? "Is everything OK, Davy?" kind Sam asked. "Did you know that Pete keeps stealing your sausages?"

"Everything's fine," Davy
replied quickly. "I'm just tired.
I think I'll have an early night."

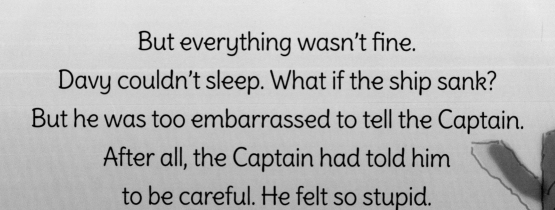

But everything wasn't fine.
Davy couldn't sleep. What if the ship sank?
But he was too embarrassed to tell the Captain.
After all, the Captain had told him
to be careful. He felt so stupid.

At first light, he snuck carefully out of his hammock, taking care not to wake Pete, and went down to the hold.

He opened the hatch to find the hold
full of water! The *Golden Duck* rolled
slowly in the stormy sea. They were sinking.
"I've got to own up," he said to himself.

Bravely, he went to see the Captain.

"I'm sorry, Captain," Davy began in a rush.
"But yesterday I dropped a cannonball and
it caused a leak, but I didn't tell you and now
the hold is full of water and I'm very, very sorry."

"Blistering barnacles.
This is terrible.
ALL HANDS ON DECK!"
the Captain cried out.

The other pirates came running,
rubbing their eyes.
 "What is it, Captain?" Pete asked.
The Captain told them what had happened.

"I'm very, very, very sorry," Davy said.
"No time to feel sorry," shouted
the Captain. "We need to save the ship!"

"Nell, dive down and plug the leak,"
the Captain ordered. "Pete and Sam,
start baling the hold. Davy, you come with me."

Nell dived down and plugged the leak
with an old pair of bloomers.

Pete and Sam baled water with huge buckets.

Davy trimmed the sails while the Captain turned the wheel, sailing them into calmer waters. Working together as a team, the pirates saved the ship!

"I'm sorry I dropped the cannonball,"
Davy said afterwards.
"We all make mistakes," Nell said,
still dripping with seawater.
"I needed a bath anyway."

"I should have said 'I did it' straightaway,"
Davy said, eyes down.
"Yes, you should have," the Captain agreed.
"But your bravery in owning up saved the ship."

"And, now that we've had all that water sloshing in the hold," the Captain continued, "we'll have the cleanest cannonballs on the seven seas!"

NOTES FOR PARENTS AND TEACHERS

Pirate Pals

The books in the *Pirate Pals* series are designed to help children recognize the virtues of generosity, honesty, politeness and kindness. Reading these books will show them that their actions and behavior have a real effect on people around them, helping them to recognize what is right and wrong, and to think about what to do when faced with difficult choices.

Pirates Can Be Honest

Pirates Can Be Honest is intended to be an engaging and enjoyable read for children aged 4-7. The book will help them recognize why it's important to be honest and that owning up is not only the right thing to do, but is the easiest choice in the long term.

Teaching children to be honest will take time and is likely to be an ongoing lesson for many years. The natural inclination of many children is to deny responsibility and seek to escape blame. Very young children may even tell fibs for entertainment value. On the other hand, children sometimes tend to tell the complete, unblemished truth even when it's not required. It's important that children learn that being honest should be tempered by manners.

Admonishing children who make mistakes, hurt one another, or damage things is a reasonable and correct approach, but it does leave children feeling anxious about bringing such transgression to the attention of an adult. It is important to reinforce the notion that honesty is a virtue in itself and that it can help to mitigate the damage caused. Make a point of thanking the child for their honesty. Explain that it doesn't make it right, but that owning up will certainly reduce the severity of the punishment.

Suggested follow-up activities

Ask the child to put him or herself in the position of Davy when he discovers the dropped cannonball has caused a leak. How does he feel when he wakes to find the ship is in real danger? What is the result of Davy's confession? Discuss how the crew react. Why do they think the Captain decides to not punish Davy?

Take time to explain what honesty is, and what a lie is. Try to instill a desire to do the right thing. Make a values chart listing all the virtues you and the child can think of. Put a sticker on the chart every time they are honest and display one of the virtues listed.

Notice and praise acts of honesty, however minor. Say "I'm pleased you were honest and told me you spilled the drink. Now let's clean this up together." Some children who learn the value of honesty can go through a phase of telling tales. Make a point of explaining about personal responsibility. It can be difficult for a child to judge when to tell an adult about misbehaving peers and when to keep out of it! Explain that taking responsibility sometimes means trying to sort matters out yourself.

Avoid lying to any child, even about difficult subjects like illness or death. If you make a mistake, own up! Young children watch and imitate adult behavior. Tell them what you are going to do and why. For example, "I broke Mrs. Smith's favorite vase. I'll tell her as soon as she gets here and buy her a new one."

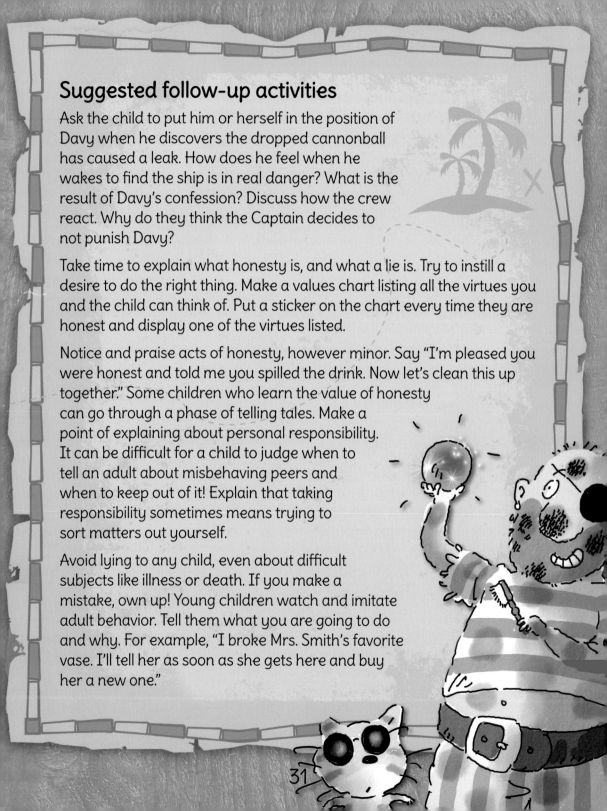

BOOKS TO SHARE

Come Clean, Carlos: Tell the Truth (You Choose)
by Sarah Eason (Wayland, 2013)

The *You Choose* series explores dilemmas that all children face.
Amusing and simple multiple-choice questions encourage children to look at
different ways to resolve situations and decide which choice they would make,
while helping the character in the book choose the RIGHT thing to do.

I Didn't Do It!: A Book About Telling the Truth (Our Emotions)
by Sue Graves (Watts, 2013)

Poppy doesn't always tell the truth at home. She doesn't always tell the truth
at school either. Now she's getting other children into trouble. Can she learn
that it's better to own up than to tell a lie?

It's Wasn't Me!
by Brian Moses (Wayland, 2008)

This amusing picture book, also illustrated by Mike Gordon, looks at why we
tell lies and how telling lies leads to trouble. It also considers the gray area
of telling a white lie, coping with angry feelings when
people tell lies about you, and having the courage
to be honest. This book is one of a series that
helps children to develop their own value
system and make responsible decisions.
Notes for parents and teachers show how
ideas in the books can be used as starting
points for further discussion, at home,
or in the classroom.